To My Dear friends — Enjoy + Peace — Blessings, Paul Hebert

Return to Eden

Paul Edgar Hebert

PublishAmerica
Baltimore

ISBN: 1-60703-849-8
PUBLISHED BY PUBLISHAMERICA, LLLP
www.publishamerica.com
Baltimore

Printed in the United States of America

In memory of our troops lost in all wars since the beginning.

Time is only now—the past only a moment before, the future only one step ahead.

Acknowledgments

I wish to thank my wife, Carolyn, for all the nights she spent waiting for me to join her in the living room, or to be by her side while I worked on the manuscript. She has always been my love and my inspiration to come into the "Light."

I also thank my daughter, Mary, who volunteered to edit the manuscript, and did it with such grace and joy that it appeared painless when I know that my writing can be a grammatical nightmare. I truly appreciate her love and support in this effort.

I am designating 10% of royalty checks received from PublishAmerica to the care of Veterans at Champ Homes, a program of the Housing for All Corporation, Cape Cod, Massachusetts. On the web at: www.champhouse.org.

It was the kind of darkness that extracts even the light inside of you, makes you feel cold, alone and by these facts, a seeker of light and others. It was to that purpose of finding the warmth of light and others that he made his way up the incline to a clearing with an unusual light.

Captain Drake approached the lighted area with extreme caution and apprehension. There were no large areas that could conceal an enemy combatant or an overly zealous friendly defendant. The area appeared an oasis that would attract anyone in the darkness of unknowing and searching to this point, from which they could re-orient themselves. The Captain certainly felt in need of understanding. What had taken place and why was he no longer in familiar territory?

Drake was a man of average height and weight. He looked as you would expect a professional soldier to present who had worked his way through the ranks and who had survived any number of campaigns. The Captain positioned himself and peered into the darkness. He waited for something to take the place of the stillness, to re-awaken a sense of time… He sensed that time was stuck in a now moment, without past or future. It was just at this moment that he became aware of the sounds of battle, with the occasional flashes of explosions on the very distant horizon. Had he traveled away from the conflict? Or had the battle moved in another direction, leaving him behind?

"Permission to approach?" A voice broke into the silence from beyond the perimeter of the area and of the Captain's thoughts. He was very much aware that those in the dark outside the circle could see him in the lighted area, while he could not see them. A scary thought.

Instinct took control and the Captain pulled the revolver from its holster, but in a gesture of acceptance, kept himself from pointing it in the direction of the request. He shouted, "Identify yourself."

"I am Private First Class Hebert. May I approach?"

"Come into the light, slowly," ordered Drake.

Private Hebert was a younger man. His uniform was bloodied from battle, and his bayonet was plainly visible in its sheath. "Captain, may I rest here awhile, wherever we are? I must have walked miles to get here. When everything went dark, this was the only light on the horizon, so I came here."

The Captain moved slowly toward the PFC while looking him over. "I am Captain Drake. Can't seem to remember my unit name, number or base for that matter. Everything went dark for me also, and the only thing I could see was this pinpoint of light, so I made my way here. What unit are you attached to, Private?"

The Private came to attention as if remembering whom he was talking to and made a salute of sorts. "Sir, I can't recall my unit's name or our mission. I'm sorry, Sir." Captain Drake made a half-hearted salute back.

"It's OK, Private. I don't think we need to be standing on any military formality here. It is as if..." his voice trailed off. "Who's there? Show yourself. Who are you?" The Captain moved back to the opposite side of the lighted area, while the Private moved to the other side, as if to form a double team position strategy.

"I am Sergeant Murphy. May I approach?"

Captain Drake, feeling more in charge than when he was alone, commanded, "Slowly Sergeant. Come into the light."

The Sergeant walked carefully into the area, and also showed evidence of surviving a battle, his uniform tattered and bloodied. Murphy was clearly an experienced line soldier; he saluted in a matter of fact manner. "I am happy to find someone alive. I've walked for miles to this one spot of light after everything went dark. It's good to get here, wherever we are."

He acknowledged the Private, while the Captain smiled, "Welcome, Sergeant, but we really don't know where we are. This is Private Hebert. We don't suppose you know what unit you are with?"

While the flashes of battle continued beyond their hearing, the Sergeant leaned against a large rock to rest himself. "No Sir, I tried to remember as I walked, but can't recall much at all. We were involved with very heavy fighting, fierce fighting. Everything went black and I saw this light. I crawled for a while, and then realized I could walk pretty well and headed uphill, in the direction of this light. I wondered about what my mission had been, or my unit, but could not remember a thing. I decided it wasn't important. I just wanted to reach this light. Reaching this point seemed like a new mission for me."

Drake took on a more relaxed, yet pensive air, as he reached out to shake hands with the Sergeant. The three seemed to try to become more emotionally and physically comfortable. "It seems the same for Private Hebert and me. I'm Captain Drake."

Responding to a sound in the darkness, the Private exclaimed, "Listen, do you hear that?"

The Captain took charge once more. "Who's there? Identify yourself."

No less than three voices broke the silence. First a man responded, "Specialist Tobey"

...Followed by a female voice, "Specialist Gomez"

...And finally I called out, "Lieutenant Smith."

Specialist Tobey was quick to add, "Who are you?"

To which the Captain responded, "I'm Captain Drake, and where are we is a better question. Come on and join us in the light. This is turning out to be one heck of a party." We three new arrivals were all in tattered and bloodied uniforms, but were walking well. We took a brief moment to survey the area while I shook hands with the Captain, who continued, "Welcome to the twilight zone. I assume you, like us, were part of the battle over there until you became separated from your units."

I spoke for our little group. "I guess so. I can't really say. I don't remember much, except one minute feeling like I was totally engaged in some struggle, and then nothing to do other than to come here. I met the Specialists in the dark as we each were advancing up the hill toward this lighted area."

I no sooner finished my report when the Sergeant yelled out, "Who's there?"

"Corporal Cohen. May I approach?" came the reply.

The Sergeant continued with, "Sure, the more the merrier!" Into our growing circle came our newest member, with the same bloodied uniform, coming from the direction of the battle. His arrival caused us to realize that the flashes seemed less, and farther away.

"Sir, I became separated from my unit, and the only thing I could see was this..."

Almost as one, the group sounded off in a joking moment of levity, "I saw this light!" The Captain smiled compassionately at the Corporal. "It is a familiar experience for each of us, Corporal. We also don't remember much about our units, our mission or what we were engaged in at the time it all went black. We aren't standing on too much formality, so just introduce yourself around and try and make yourself comfortable."

The Corporal grabbed all of our attention when he all of a sudden exclaimed, "Sir, I do remember one objective."

The Captain became visibly excited at the potential of even the smallest amount of information, and with a hopeful voice toward the Corporal asked, "Objective, Corporal?" The Corporal immediately realized he did not have what the group was desperate for, but he completed his thought.

"Yes Sir. The main objective is to stay alive...always, to just stay alive!" His voice drifted off as he recognized that he had not been able to bring any closure on how we had all come to be at this spot and at this time.

"Who's there?" The Captain was on his feet again. "I thought I heard something out there. If this isn't the strangest thing that one minute we are in some action and then each of us finds ourselves coming to this one, lighted area. Why can't we remember our units, our objectives? Hell, I cannot even remember who we are fighting."

I felt empathy for the Captain, who appeared strained in thought and confused. I finally made the suggestion, "Perhaps we are all shell shocked."

Specialist Mary Gomez, our only medic and female, attempted to shed some insight into our situation. "Selective memories of name and rank are one thing, but not to remember our units or positions would seem a bit much. Unless... Are any of you pretending so as not to reveal any information that might be helpful to the enemy? Since, for all you know, the enemy might be putting this whole thing on to get one of us to talk." She went on, "I can tell by the looks on your faces that no one here buys that idea. You all find this as agitating and foolish as I do. Maybe we all come from the same unit, but we should remember each other if that's the case. Perhaps remembering some things is not really what is important here after all."

"Who is out there?"

"Did you hear that?"

Captain Drake peered into the darkness.

Specialist Tobey felt the need to express his feelings next. "Sir, I am in communications. As I recall, I felt our situation was desperate and very intense. I believe I was calling for support and, personally, I was praying when, Boom! Nothing but blackness and this lighted spot."

The Captain continued not to hear the comments from the Specialist, as he said loudly, "I can feel you out there. Come forward and identify yourself. This is Captain Drake."

A young sounding voice replied, "Private Jacques, Sir."

The Captain immediately appeared to become fatherly in his response, "Okay, Jacques. Come and join us."

After a very short silence, the Private responded with an air of trust, and seeking compassion from the officer, said, "I can't, Sir."

Our medic was quick to inquire if the Private was injured and volunteered to go to him. Captain Drake continued his apparent role of caring for the troops by asking, "Jacques, are you hurt?"

Private Jacques responded immediately, "No Sir, only my pride."

"Well then, come here," responded Drake.

Now, with hesitation, the Private softly spoke the words, "Sir, I am naked!"

In disbelief, Captain Drake's voice was raised slightly as he returned with a clear question. "What did you say?"

Private Jacques did not need to shout, since the silence around us was unimaginable. Every word seemed spoken from center stage with the finest acoustics in the world. "Last I remember, I was taking a shower, and then the lights went out. I came toward this light—but I am very naked."

"Well Jacques," replied Drake, "you can stay there if you want, but it feels creepy having you in the dark. No, damn it man! We are all soldiers here. Come forward and join us."

Slowly young Jacques entered from the darkness into the light of our circle, naked, embarrassed, unharmed, young and handsome. There was wholesomeness in his attempt to cover his privates with his left hand as he quickly acknowledged the Captain with a right hand salute. The rest of the gathered soldiers laughed lightly, wearing expressions of appreciation for the awkwardly humorous situation.

Specialist Mary Gomez broke the uncomfortable moment with, "This is an easy check for injuries. You look fine, Jacques, obviously not a scratch on you. I was starting to think that, possibly, we were all dead and in the tunnel of light. But you are really very fine in every way."

I was easily one of the largest men in the group, so I took off my shirt and handed it to Jacques with the hope of helping the young man to relax. "There you go Private. This should cover you, lessen the embarrassment a bit." I regretted the word as it passed my lips, since I knew there had to be at least one joker in the group.

Sure enough, Private Hebert, with a juvenile smile, blurted out, "Bare-ass-ment, get it?"

Jacques only responded with, "Thank you, Sir."

As the poor kid turned away from the group to put on the covering of my shirt, I was not prepared for the horror of seeing that his back was so totally blown out. I began to turn away so as not to become sick and I saw the astonished look on every face. Perhaps the most anguished look was now coming from the recent comedian, Private Hebert.

Medic Gomez, deflated, exclaimed, "Well, so much for that theory."

Corporal Cohen seemed thrown off balance by the revelation of Private Jacques obviously fatal injuries. Wanting to break the tension, he took the opportunity to resume talk, and noted, "Hey, the fighting has stopped. Listen."

Private Tobey commented, "All is quiet on the front."

The small group of isolated soldiers listened and looked in the direction of the former battlefield. Private Hebert interjected, "This is F'in strange. If I weren't here, I wouldn't believe any of this. I keep thinking this is some sort of dream, that none of this is real, that none of you are real and that any minute I'll wake up from this nightmare."

Corporal Cohen spoke up, "I'm in reconnaissance work and I really want to know where we are and know the territory and the situation. I think this is more than a dream, and unless I am very wrong, we are all starting to realize that we are in some way trapped here, or at least brought here for some purpose."

"Specialist Gomez, as the medic, you need to check us out. Are we alive or F'in dead?" was the input from Sergeant Murphy.

Captain Drake seemed to come back from his thoughts. "Good idea, Sergeant. Specialist, check us out."

Medic Gomez went immediately to Lieutenant Smith, in his bloody tee shirt, and felt for a pulse. "Sir, if you have a pulse, I am not finding it. Could you remove your shirt?" As the obedient Lieutenant Smith removed his shirt, there were clearly several apparent bullet holes on his upper torso.

The first response came from Sergeant Murphy. "Well, seeing is believing!" There was no longer any need for the Medic to make the rounds, as each member of the group began to remove shirts and do self examinations of body parts to realize that they were, in fact, all quite dead.

A rather shaken Private Jacques queried the Medic with, "But Specialist, you said I was fine."

The Medic, as gently as possible and looking Jacques straight in the eye said, "Sorry, Buddy. When you turned around, well, you have no back. You are as gone as the rest of us. It does explain why no one is complaining about pain. We apparently have lost the ability to experience physical pain."

Corporal Cohen was caught up in the emotion of the revelation. In his need to express a spiritual concept, he added, "I believe that I will see the good things of the Lord in the land of the living." He said this as each pensive person put their shirts back on. A very solemn atmosphere fell upon the group.

In an attempt to bring everyone back into the moment, the Captain suggested, "Well the good news is that I don't think we are in the Army anymore."

Corporal Cohen replied, "Yes, but there is a reason why we are here, brought out of the darkness to this place."

To which Private Tobey added, "Out of the darkness I have called you."

Continuing to quote scripture, Corporal Cohen offered, "I have called you by name. I, The Lord, will set you free. I have written your name upon My hand."

Private Tobey quickly confirmed, "They who were in darkness have seen a great light."

"Enough of this shit." The outburst came from Sergeant Murphy. "If I weren't already dead, you both would be killing me with this crap. I doubt that we are dead. There has got to be a rational explanation."

The Captain touched his revolver. In his frustration, he responded to Sergeant Murphy with, "Ah! What if I use my revolver and see if you are any deader after I put another round into you, Sergeant?"

Specialist Gomez supported the Captain, explaining, "I don't think that will be necessary Captain. Put your fingers in the bullet holes, Sergeant. Feeling is even surer than seeing." It finally came to each member of the group that they are indeed dead.

Private Tobey spoke up, "This must be the light that people talk about coming to when they die. I expected a tunnel of super white light and moving quickly toward heaven."

Sergeant Murphy sarcastically responded, "Well, I think we got stuck at a station."

Captain Drake addressed the group with an air of giving up command. "Let's drop the bravado and share our first names and something about ourselves, OK? I'm Peter, married, was married I should say. I am—correction—I should say I was professional military. I'm thirty-five years old and since we have been quoting scripture, let's share our religious affiliation if you want. I happen to be a Methodist."

Private Hebert appeared anxious to be next, so he jumped right in with, "I'm Philip and I'm nineteen years old." Appearing on the verge of tears, he was quick to correct himself, as Peter had, by adding, "I was nineteen. I never had the chance to get married. I was raised as a Lutheran."

Sergeant Murphy was sitting right next to Philip, so he seemed like the natural choice to speak up next. "I guess I'm your doubting Thomas. Listen, I am twenty-five years old and a hard nosed atheist, so I hate to bust any of your bubbles, but I doubt you would be with me in any tunnel of light."

"I'm Matthew Smith, twenty-three years young, married to the most beautiful woman in the world with two great kids. I'm the last practicing Catholic of my brothers and sisters, and so far having a belief in Jesus has kept me going so I could get through this hell of a war and get back to my wife and kids."

Corporal Cohen seemed eager to speak right after Matthew expressed the support he got from his faith. He jumped in with, "I'm Moses, and I am proud to be Jewish. I am only twenty-two and I miss my wife and child so very much."

In an almost excited manner, at finding a kindred spirit, it was Private Jacques who responded, "I am Jewish also. My name is Adam, no less, and at twenty years old, my old Rabbi would be quick to shake his lowered head, repeating over and over, 'So young to die, so many and so young.'"

"I'm John Tobey, nineteen years old, and a Bible carrying Baptist."

Medic Gomez surprised no one with the revelation that she was a mother when she spoke up. "I'm Mary, married to a real charmer, a professional military guy.

We have a beautiful daughter that I had to leave when they activated my unit. I was raised a Catholic, but now I enjoy many different faith expressions."

As Mary finished talking, the light around the group seemed to simply go out for a very brief moment, and before anyone could even respond, the light came back with a bit more intensity than before. Moses appeared almost astonished that a physical event had taken place, and shared his thoughts to the group as though they might have somehow missed it. "WOW! What was that? Did you feel that? A flash of darkness, and then here we are again!"

Philip was talking next, but still clearly in his own thoughts as he spoke, "It was more than just dark and then light again. Something happened. I feel different. As a matter of fact, I wasn't aware that I really wasn't feeling anything before the light went out and came back on, and now I feel very different. Feelings and thoughts are pouring into me."

John acted like he needed to keep this conversation going in the same direction by jumping right in with, "I feel so different too! Things are pouring back into my brain, and I believe somehow a great piece of this puzzle is coming alive in my head. I sense somehow that someone is communicating with my mind."

Peter was on his feet. "It is more than with my mind. It is deep in my consciousness. No, it is even deeper than the conscious mind, it is something very deep that I don't think I have ever paid much attention to."

Adam appeared nervous, and added, "When the light flashed off for that second, I found myself in more darkness than I have ever experienced, and I felt some thing inside of me change, or maybe something that woke me up. Something happened to me that I think is not over."

Doubting Thomas saw his opportunity to get his say. "Something happened to me too, but I'm not going to buy into any of this crap. I didn't think that dead people could be affected by anything once they are dead, let alone to start thinking they are experiencing something new. Of course, I admit that I have never been dead before."

Philip responded, "I don't feel like a lot changed for me with the light flashing off and back on. I mean, I don't seem to remember a lot more than I did before the flash, but something did happen. I believe it is still going on, I mean, inside of me. I think I am about to find out why I am here, and I don't like it. I am afraid of what I'm going to find out. I feel it isn't good."

Mary smiled at Philip. "I know what you mean, Philip, but I am not afraid. Somehow I think it is going to be good. Somehow we are about to grow, and to heal. Perhaps you are right to be afraid, and there might be a lot of pain and discomfort, but I believe there is healing for us that is right in the air around us."

"WOW! I agree, Mary. Somehow the flash was a sign of good news. At least something happened. We all feel different, and that's at least something. Don't get me wrong, I'm still afraid and confused, but you know what I'm feeling right now? Well, I shouldn't say anything."

Philip insisted, "No, say it Matthew, I feel it too. Yes, it is what we are here for, right here and now."

Matthew continued, "I sense this is a judgment time for each of us. Whatever we were doing just before everything went black and we came to this light is what this is all about. What we were doing is the summation of our life, and we need to reveal it, understand it, and then we will be free. At least this is what I am thinking."

John joined in, "I can't believe that what I have believed all my life might actually be going to happen. I was raised to believe that we would be preparing a way for God to come not only into our own life, but that through us God would be revealed to the world. As a Baptist I believed in preparing the way of the Lord."

Of course Thomas had had enough. "No way, Jose! Not going there, no way in Hell am I going to get wrapped up in this garbage. My life has gone along just fine without getting into all this God stuff. The way I see it, God doesn't need me and I don't need God and the world has done just fine. Don't get me wrong, I do have a relationship with God, and that is that we don't have a relationship. It has gotten me this far." The light flashed off and on again just as Thomas finished speaking, and the response of the group was as intense as the first time.

Moses seemed excited, "Another sign from above, no doubt. I expect we will all grow again from this flash. We seem to be crossing a desert of our thoughts. We have something to learn about ourselves in this journey."

"I do feel a lot different, and things are getting clearer and clearer," added John. "I believe we have an opportunity here to look at our last moments of life and see ourselves as God sees us. I guess it is about understanding how God does see us and now we see ourselves through God's eyes."

Mary noticed that Peter had his head in his hands and appeared to be crying. "Peter, are you OK? Peter, Peter!"

"In the last flash it all came back to me. I remember exactly what I was doing when it all went black. A young soldier was in a panic. He was deserting his post and was moving toward the back lines. He was crying, but I grabbed him by the collar and pushed him against a large rock and ordered him to stop and return to his post. I demanded to know where his weapon was and the little bastard told me he had dropped it when he decided to run. I slapped the S.O.B. as hard as I could across the face, screaming at him that he had left the rest of us to do his work. He just stood there scared and shaking, and then with tears pouring down from his pathetic little face he said, 'What work is that Captain? To send as many others back home in body bags before I get put into one? Whatever is left of me after I'm blown to hell?'"

Mary truly looked with compassion toward the officer in charge of this troop of soldiers somewhere between heaven and hell. "And then what did you do, Peter? I think whatever you did is why you are here with us now."

Peter continued, "He was deserting. Our unit was falling apart. We had a job to do and I couldn't just let him go. He could fall into enemy hands. Hell, if he got hurt we would have to get him help, and I couldn't let him just run away. He was begging me to let him go. I did what I had to do. Other soldiers were watching, and if I let him go they all would have turned and run. I pulled out my revolver and pointed it at his head. He said, 'Go ahead, I'd rather you kill me for a reason, than someone who doesn't know me or doesn't know any more why he is trying to kill me than I know why I'm trying to kill him.' I had this feeling like I've never had before, and I wanted to do one thing more than I wanted my own life at that moment, but instead I pulled the trigger." At this revelation, Peter fell to his knees, burying his head in his hands once again, as he said, "I saw him smile as I shot him. It was like it was finally over for him, and as he fell I fired a second round into his dead body."

Mary had moved closer to Peter, and placing her hand on his shoulder, asked, "Peter, would you do anything different, now that you can see this from a distance?"

Peter looked up with tears running down his face. "That kid could have been my son. He was so afraid. He begged me to let him go, and I shot him. I keep hearing Jesus saying, 'What father would give his child a stone if they asked for bread?' The kid was begging me for a chance and I killed him."

John seemed inspired to ask what we all were wondering. "Peter, you said there was something you wanted to do more than anything, but instead you pulled the trigger. What was that thing?"

Peter seemed relieved to be able to share his strong feeling. "I wanted to be a father to that boy. I wanted to just hug him and tell him everything would be OK. I wish I had been able to calm him down and stay with him. I wish I had died with him."

Moses stood up, and for the first time, it appeared that he had a serious head injury, earlier mistaken as just a bloody open wound. He moved slowly toward Peter as he began to speak. "I see clearly now why I am here. Peter, I was in a tunnel of light going toward a beautiful field, and a very gentle looking person said that I had one more thing to do before I could go on. I was instructed to move toward this lighted spot because there was one person I would need to escort into the Promised Land with me. At the last flash it came back to me that I had been rescued from my fear and confusion by someone who wanted to love me but couldn't because of his sense of duty. I am here as a son to you, Peter. Thank you for being my way out of killing anymore. Back there I had a thought of you as my father, as you pointed the revolver to my head. If it is okay with you, I'll take that hug now?"

Just as the older and younger man hugged, the light flashed once again, and when we could see clearly again, Peter and Moses were no longer with us.

Adam stood up wearing only the shirt I had given him, and he sounded unsure of himself and still embarrassed. "I was naked so I was ashamed. It was before the artillery attack. We had had three days of quiet. There were no signs of enemy troops and we had rigged up a water bag so we could take turns taking our first shower in months. I felt like I was in heaven, and then everything went dark. Next thing I knew I was walking in a beautiful field with a stream. I could see and hear birds. Two people in white robes were approaching me, smiling and welcoming me. I realized I was naked and began walking in the opposite direction, trying to cover myself. The two called out loudly, 'Welcome, Adam. Come with us. We were expecting you. Come on.' But I yelled back, 'Stay away. Leave me alone.' I turned and started running, and then it was dark and all I could see was this lighted area, so I came here. I realize now I ran from heaven, or the Garden of Eden. I was naked so I felt shame. I ran from heavenly beings because I was naked. Does this story sound a little familiar to anyone?"

Mary appeared so peaceful, and she smiled as she began to speak. "Adam, I have a theory about what happened in the Garden of Eden that long time ago, and I don't think much has changed. What if the first original sin was not some specific disobedience, but the beginning of real pride and arrogance? What if the all powerful and loving Creator, who was so happy to share life and creation with these newly created children, found that all of a sudden Adam and Eve had made clothing for themselves? You know how saddened we are when we believe we have made something beautiful or a surprise for someone special, only to be crushed when they are disappointed with our special gift, or worse, they reject our present altogether? Well, how do you think God felt when His children hid from Him and said they were naked? Imagine this hurt Creator saying, 'Who told you that you were naked?' I imagine they added insult to injury by their pride and arrogance when they expressed how awful this sexual process was, and why did the Creator come up with such an idea?

Sounds like our first parents thought they were smarter than the Creator, and nothing has changed in thousands of years."

Mary continued to look gently and lovingly toward Adam, who was taking in every word and appearing more relaxed. "Adam, some religious leaders have acted like the body was bad, and sex worse. The natural beauty of our bodies constantly was a thing of disgust, with only the master painters or sculptors allowed to show it off as art. We took a gift from the Creator and turned it into a thing of disgust and shame. You responded to the heavenly creatures as you were programmed all your life. You continued, Adam, like your namesake, to insult God. You rejected the Garden of Eden because that is what you were trained to do from birth. I have believed this for a long time. We have rejected and criticized God's very creation. Now I know why I am here. If you are ready, Adam, I would like to walk you back into Eden." Mary walked over to Adam and smiled ever so gently into his relaxed face.

Adam seemed like a new person, and a glow seemed to envelop him as he spoke. "Mary, you are more than a medic, you are a spiritual healer. Thank you for that insight. I am truly sorry that I was ever ashamed of God's creation or thought I knew better than God. I realize that the serpent or the devil had done the same thing when he believed that he knew better than a loving Creator. Thanks for walking me back home." Adam removed my shirt and dropped it on the ground. With a cherub's smile, he continued, "I'd better leave this here, I want to be recognized for who I am—a created child of God, who appreciates and likes how the Creator made me." Adam reached for Mary's hand, and as they both turned to walk into what appeared to be a lighted path, Adam said, "Oh Lord, here I am!" Before anyone could respond, we again experienced the evaporation of the light into the dark, and its return that seemed a little brighter.

The new light found Philip pacing back and forth, obviously ready to speak, with

an aura of horror and anger. "Well my situation isn't as easy as accepting my body or sexuality. The last flash brought it all back to me. We were in fierce hand to hand combat. We were being overrun and I had pulled out my bayonet. I was fighting for my life with this guy, and finally I had him pinned down and my bayonet moving toward just under his breastbone, and he was holding back my hand with all his strength. I had the advantage of my body weight, so I slowly pushed down with my body. I heard the pop as my bayonet entered his body, and I felt his body stiffen. I looked right into his eyes. He was my age, as dirty and as tired as I was, as lonely and afraid, and I killed him. He was somebody's son, brother or father. He could have been my brother, but I killed him. You know what was worse? I believe I heard him say just as I stuck him, 'I love you.' I went mad with rage that he would say that, maybe because I was taking him out of his misery. I don't know, but I didn't have time to think about it. But you know what I did?"

Philip was tense, filled with his anger from just re-telling the incident, and I thought he was going to explode, but to my surprise, he went on recounting the event. "As the knife got closer to his heart I twisted it. My steel blade in his chest, and I hated him for being there, for my being there, and then everything went dark. I hope one of his friends got the satisfaction of blowing me away." Philip seemed exhausted by the revelation and he fell to his knees, burying his face into his hands. We couldn't help but really empathize with him. What could we say to him? I was relieved when John, who was sitting on a rock, spoke up. "Do you believe, Philip, that I am in the Father and the Father is in Me? Jesus said that to His disciple Philip, according to John in Chapter 14. I know my Bible, but can't say I have lived it. I can quote chapter and verse, but it has been a lot of lip service, I guess. I imagine I am here because knowing the Bible and living it are two entirely different things. It is like putting fuel in the engine, but not turning it on. Nothing happens. As you spilled your guts here, Philip, the words of Jesus burned into my heart. 'Love your enemies, do good to those who persecute you, forgive one another, have brotherly love for everyone and turn the other cheek.' Jesus was consistent and just like Adam's naked thing, we always settled for the alternative interpretation to fit our purposes. Whether that poor kid you killed was thankful you were putting him out of his misery, or was happy he wasn't killing you, or he realized that you could have been brothers at another place or time, he may have been expressing an idea that could have changed the world, simply by saying I love you. Jesus said, 'They will know that you are my disciples by your love for one another.' How did we just push that aside like it was a joke? I'm serious. We have done anything but love one another through the centuries after Jesus, with all sorts of excuses and reasons. Millions and millions have died because we ignored the command to love God and neighbor. I had hoped to make a difference in this world when I was growing up, but then life just got caught up with making ends meet and doing what I was told. Patriotism was given a higher place than obedience to God. Every rational reason was given why the fifth commandment, Thou shall not kill, was not meant to be taken to mean you could not hate and kill your enemies. The Church was fast to proclaim defense of church and country and faith as exceptions to the teachings of Jesus. 'Forgive them, Father, for they know not what they are doing.' Jesus knew what He was saying when He said that, and we haven't known what we were doing for centuries."

"But I'm not gay, and I hated that I thought he said he loved me." Philip was up on his feet, ready to work out an understanding of this pain that now gripped him, mostly in his heart. "Yet, would it be wrong if I loved him? I am so sorry I killed him."

John left the relaxed position of sitting on the rock and advanced a bit toward Philip. "'For God's ways are not our ways. I am the way, the truth and the life.' That is what Jesus left us with, and we just don't want to accept it. Religions have used their influence over people for various reasons, but Jesus was very clear that in the final judgment, it is love that will rule. Religions have been the ally of governments and movements, they have tried to control people and God, with a lot of success, I would say. Who are we to judge? Almighty God and Jesus warned us not to judge others, but we do it all the time. I heard you worry about even thinking for a second that you might be gay, as if that would be somehow worse than killing another human being. It was drilled into us that as soldiers we were defending our country, we have the right to kill. That seems of little comfort now that we have been killed, and so are seeing things very differently in this light. Did we fight as hard for peace and love as we trained and worked at being killing machines for our way of life? Strange to be talking about a way of life when we are dead and are now questioning how we did our jobs so well killing others. Loving another person makes us human and obedient to God. It has nothing to do with sexuality. What are the churches going to talk about in heaven, when sex is not an issue?"

Philip was sobbing again, and looked at John with begging eyes that asked for understanding and forgiveness. "I am so sorry I hated him as I killed him."

John looked with compassion and tenderness to Philip, as he gently responded, "You know what is sad? We become numb to killing. Since Cain killed Abel, we have been killing each other. Jesus tried even to His death to show us a better way, but we are filled with pride and arrogance. We have a love affair with hate, prejudice, discrimination and killing. You know what I realized? We humans can watch hours of violence in movies or plays, read of atrocities, murders and even watch a man cut another man to pieces, but we are repulsed if we see a man kiss another man. It has bothered me all my life, and now I know why I am here in this light with you. Our walk to God was stopped because we both needed to come to terms with this issue. Who is my neighbor? Can I really show that I am a follower of the Lord by really loving? Can I take God at His word and trust with all my heart that we are one in God? This is not some corny exercise here, or some religious service. We are dead and God has seen fit to give us a chance to choose Him or darkness. God forgives all our offenses, but we are free to choose Him or our negative self-judgment. Our fears and hates can destroy love, but you know not even the most powerful person or bomb can destroy love. Love is eternal. God is Love."

As John finished his thoughts, he walked to a bent over Philip and placed his hands on Philip's shoulders. He addressed him with a smile. "Philip, in the name of love, I am your brother and I love you. The brother you killed loves you and God loves us all. Will you walk with me into the Kingdom of God? Will you allow love to triumph today, or pride and death?"

Philip appeared exhausted from his soul-searching experience, as if he had just completed climbing a mountain; however, he replied with enthusiastic warmth and serenity. "I have denied love's authority over me based on fear and rigid beliefs. I will walk with you. Thank you." As they walked toward the edge of the lighted area, it was Philip who stopped, and gently said, "John." I saw them turn to each other, and with a kiss we experienced once again the flash of darkness and the rapid return of the light.

It was now just Thomas and I, and he spoke first. "It is a miracle. No, it is two miracles. Actually, it is three miracles. As a Sergeant, I have never shut up this long before. As an atheist, I have never experienced this much God talk. And as a person, I am truly amazed by what I have witnessed. You know what turned me against believing in God all these years was that religions preached their version of God and the people who went to the different religions didn't really seem to be any better than the rest of us. Finally, I see dead people living what they were taught about God. I have really seen some sharing, caring and a love for God and neighbor. Not just talking about it, but living it in the reality of death and choosing life over darkness."

Being the last two left in the light was very interesting, and I wondered what our issues would be. Thomas certainly opened the door for me to just be myself. "I must say it was refreshing to see hearts of stone replaced with real human hearts of flesh. We both got to see dried out bones of laws replaced with the new flesh of the words of God, taken with sincere hearts." Thomas had this great big smile as he continued to express himself. "Well, my mother always said I was the doubting Thomas of the family, and I lived up to it. I am glad that God gave me this opportunity to experience this and to finally believe. The religions did get the basic message out to the people, and they kept God's message available, but it is faith and love like I have seen here that makes it all real. It is love that gives faith life. My Lord and my God!" The light flashed before I could even respond, and just like that I was the only one left.

So now I was alone with my thoughts. I realized that ultimately, Jesus said we would be judged by how we took care of one another. I remembered how Jesus said, "I was hungry and you fed me, thirsty and you gave me to drink, a stranger and you took me into your homes, sick and you took care of me, in prison and you visited me and I was naked and you clothed me." As I finished my thoughts, it occurred to me that I had been able to clothe naked Adam with my shirt, and just then, pain ripped through my side where I had perceived a bullet hole when we first determined that we were dead. Now I felt very much alive—and in pain—as I grabbed at my side and felt the warmth of my own blood. Just at that moment I could see the sun was rising. The landscape around me revealed that I was on an elevated hill, with the dead and dying only yards away in every direction. Was it my one act of kindness in giving my shirt to lessen Adam's embarrassment that gave me back my life? I felt that I was being invited back to the feast of the living, but with greater insights to the power of truth and love. I realized that Thomas was right when he said that the religions kept the message of God alive through the ages, but I feared they put God in a museum, so people could remember by hearing stories about God rather than be filled with the Spirit of Who God Is—the living God of Love. I knew from the long night's experience that now I wanted to be set on fire with love in my heart for God and neighbor, to change the world, and to make a return to Eden.

I began to walk down the hill and met two medics checking for any live soldiers among the dead. We all reached Adam at the same time, and I heard one say to the other, "Lieutenant Smith, according to his shirt."

As I approached I said, "That would be me. Since the kid had nothing else, I gave him my shirt. I believe that wonderful medic holding his hand is Mary Gomez." The medics proceeded to place Mary's body on their stretcher, bringing their own to the temporary morgue, when they became aware that I was injured.

"Sir, sorry we didn't realize you are wounded, please let us take a look at you."

I put up my hand in protest. "I have been up on this hill all night. I'll get myself to the hospital tent after we carry these two to the morgue. You carry Mary and let me carry young Adam. I shared a lot more than just my shirt with these two." As we made our way down toward the emergency tents, we passed the bodies of Captain Peter Drake near that of Corporal Moses Cohen. A little further on, the body of Specialist John Tobey appeared to be protecting that of Private Philip Hebert. By himself, over a large boulder, almost appearing to be on his knees in prayer was Sergeant Thomas Murphy. His mother would be so proud of her doubting Thomas.

Epilogue

Lieutenant Matthew Smith returned home as a very changed and passion-charged man who became a public servant and advanced in the political world with stunning speed to become Mr. President. In the year 2020, he would find himself at the International Hotel Francoise in Paris, France, at the height of the International Emergency Council for Economic and Military Aid.

A French Diplomat escorts President Smith's small group to a comfortable suite and leaves the President with the Vice Presidents of Energy and the Military, promising to return later to escort the President to address the full gathered Emergency Council.

Since 2012, President Smith has worked for justice and peace, while making Constitutional changes that resulted in the creation of six vice-presidents, each with specific oversight responsibilities. The Country now stands as the economic, educational and military power of the world. Among its finest achievements is the creation of a system of solar space stations that beam abundant amounts of energy to transfer stations located on earth. Energy is free to all throughout the Country and provides a positive balance of trade through the sale of energy to other nations.

At this meeting, President Smith learns, much to his concern, that the Vice Presidents of Energy and the Military have developed the ultimate weapon. It can melt missile silo doors shut or destroy a military vehicle or missile anywhere in the world from the remote location of the space stations. It was the President's hope that the energy space project would be used only for peaceful purposes, and he is dismayed that he was never informed of the development of the weapon system. The Vice Presidents explain that when miners were trapped underground, they were able to experiment with the system to safely save the trapped miners using a concentrated energy beam. Later, they were able to practice with demolition projects that lead to outright military experiments. Just recently it was proven perfectly accurate, and they were waiting for the right time to inform President Smith of their achievement. They shared his concern over the power of the system and its potential for misuse in the wrong hands.

The meeting of the Emergency Council was to seek the assistance of the world governments, led by President Smith, to rescue a nation embroiled in civil war with several renegade generals who had their fingers on nuclear weapons and threatened to use them on any nation that would come to the aid of the embattled democracy. Not wanting to let the world know that he now possessed the ultimate weapon on the face of the Earth, but wanting to send the requested aid, he was in a quandary as to his options. The Vice President of the Military suggested that a show of force to the threatening generals could be done that would demonstrate the futility of any opposition and could be blamed on U.F.O.s. As ridiculous as the scheme appeared, with assurances that the demonstration of power could be made without loss of human life by sending a warning in advance, President Smith gave the okay.

President Smith's secretary entered the room to announce, "Sir, the President of the United States is on the line."

President Matthew Smith, veteran of war and man of peace, picked up the phone, "Hello Mr. President. Yes, we are coming to your aid. The Vice Presidents of Energy and the Military inform me that we will have resources available to you by the end of the day." He listened to the embattled President's gracious thanks for the assistance and how desperate the state of affairs had become. He also was reminded that some generals promised immediate retaliation on any nation entering the country. President Matthew

Smith, veteran of the "Light" experience on the hilltop and ever willing to give comfort, even the shirt off his back, responded, "Yes, Mr. President, we are aware of the generals, and it appears that they have angered some U.F.O.s who will communicate with them shortly. We don't expect any further hindrance from them. Yes, I didn't believe in the U.F.O.s myself, but apparently they like protecting our democracies. God Bless, Mr. President, our prayers are with you and your country."

The End

Appendix

Prayer for the Nations

Oh great God of compassion and love have mercy on us the children of Abraham who have become the Jewish, Christian and Islamic peoples. Instead of recognizing our family ties as one people blessed by Your abundant generosity from the good earth, we have squandered our resources on wars and separation, damaged the earth and killed our brothers and sisters of the other faiths. Remember Your promise to make the children of Abraham into many nations and as numerous as the stars. Please forgive our lust for power and money and call us back, through Your Spirit, into an enlightened state of harmony and love for You and all the families of Abraham. Amen

By Paul Hebert, written at Champ Homes, October 21, 2008.